WAITING FOR HEAVEN

JILL THRUSSELL

CONTENTS

1 THE WAITING ROOM

A quick glance is cast around the silent white, stark waiting room as Mikia starts to absorb her new surroundings as no explanation has been provided as to why she is there, or what exactly is about to happen to her next. Inside the waiting room, five strangers sit upon some of the chairs but they all look totally unrecognizable to her and there are absolutely no similar characteristics that Mikia can see present among any of their faces as she silently begins to inspect each one and searches for some kind of common elements. Nothing but blank expressions however, are all that are present and everyone around Mikia looks absolutely clueless as to why they are there too, from what she can see a first glance.

In fact, all that is present is a strange, eerie, quiet stillness that adorns the interior of the entire room like a blanket and as Mikia thoughtfully considers when it might end, she explores the possibility that it might actually continue indefinitely into eternity. No one it appears, has any desire to interrupt that rather unsettling silence, rip it to shreds or obliterate it completely with pleasant words, warm smiles and friendly conversation and so the silence continues. Ignorance, Mikia quickly concludes, will definitely have to be her only companion for now as she holds her thoughts quietly inside her mind and keeps her lips firmly shut as she does nothing but wait.

After what seems like an eternity of nothingness and stillness, a young woman in quite close proximity to Mikia, suddenly stretches out a hand towards her and Mikia quickly gives her a warm, friendly smile of encouragement as she rapidly tries to offer her a pleasant response. No one else inside the room however, utters a single word, makes any effort to join them or tries to exchange any pleasantries with the two as Mikia quietly concludes that the two women will definitely have to be the first to break the icy cold stillness which is present in every inch of the room around her.

"Hi, I'm Susan. Do you know why we're here?" She asks in a quiet whisper.

"Nope. I have absolutely no clue." Mikia replies as she gently shakes Susan's hand. "Hi Susan, I'm Mikia."

Rather politely, Susan offer of a hand of friendship to break the ice between them both and introduce herself seems pleasant and innocent enough but her question makes it immediately apparent that no one inside the room is any wiser than Mikia is as to why they are all actually there. Some dark, deep red gashes are engraved into each of Susan's arms as Mikia curiously casts a glance over the rest of her frame and wonders what she has been through.

Although Susan seems harmless and friendly enough, her deep scars certainly don't look very friendly at all as they give a silent indication of the severe pain that has been inflicted upon her, prior to her arrival as Mikia silently deliberates as to what could have possibly happened to her. Each item of clothing around Susan's form is torn with fresh bloodstains across every inch of the material and it appears sodden and as her scarred arms poke silently out from under the sleeves of her light pink blouse, Mikia quietly starts to speculate as to why Susan might actually be in such a physical mess.

Despite the rather messy condition of Susan's physical form however, Mikia manages to hide her inner thoughts and questions as she gives Susan another friendly smile and prepares to engage her further in conversation. After all, there really isn't much else to do and it feels polite, courteous and appropriate for Mikia to appreciate Susan's efforts as so far, she has been friendlier towards Mikia than anyone else inside the room.

"Do you think they'll tell us why we're here soon?" Mikia asks.

"I'm not sure Mikia. Whoever 'they' might be." Susan teases in response. "It's lovely to meet you though all the same, though obviously, it's not in the best of circumstances of course."

"What circumstances are those Susan? You seem to know more than I do." Mikia probes as a look of total confusion rapidly spreads out across her face. "And how long have you been waiting here?"

"Not long, I arrived just before you did actually." Susan explains.

Even though a rather tricky, tense silence returns to the room as soon as the two women fall silent once more, the women's words and friendly conversation seems to somehow break the spell of stillness as some of the other people inside the room smile and nod in response. At least two of the occupants inside the room start to inch their forms forward as they provide a clear indication of their interest in the two women's conversation and it's almost as if the weight of silence that had been sat upon each of their shoulders has just been mysteriously lifted off by Mikia and Susan's friendly exchange.

Rather unintentionally, an interest in the discussion it seems had now been stirred by the two women's friendly words and as Mikia glances at the two stranger's faces, she gives each one a warm welcoming smile as she encourages them to join the conversation. Irrespective of their interest in the conversation however, for a couple of minutes no one actually speaks at all as Mikia silently holds onto her words in the hope that they will join the discussion and then she too can converse with them. Due to Mikia's generally quite shy nature there is a slight reluctance within her to push herself forward because she is essentially in the presence of strangers and also very unsure of where she actually is, or why she is there and so she waits patiently for them to participate with the conversation voluntarily and through their own volition.

"You do know we're dead right?" A tall, handsome man in his early thirties suddenly asks.

"Oh yes, I definitely know that. My death was absolutely awful, I'll never forget it." Susan immediately replies.

The man's words quickly bring a very valid point and harsh reality to Mikia's attention and as she starts to accept the clarity of his observations, she suddenly realizes that she is too actually dead. Somehow, the man rather perceptively manages to bring their current human state to light, or lack of it and that ultimately provides Mikia with a pinprick of shock as each word starts to run rampant through the passages of her mind and tug at her thoughts.

Frustratingly for Mikia, she can barely even remember a single thing that happened to her earlier that day and the sudden discovery that she is actually dead is very unsettling as she tries to silently accept, digest and adapt to it. Death, rather strangely had paid an actual visit Mikia's life and no amount of discussion or denial could now actually change that and so she silently began to accept her present circumstances, even though being alive would have been the greatly preferred alternative.

From what Mikia can see as she glances at Susan face again in an attempt to occupy her mind and distract herself, Susan looks not a day older than twenty-five and that immediately surprises her. Death as Mikia knows however, really doesn't discriminate and so Susan's age really could not immunise her from that potential experience in life, regardless of any human, mortal technicalities. Unlike Mikia, Susan and the friendlier male, it seems both possess a far greater awareness of their own deaths that day and that intrigues Mikia slightly as she'd been absolutely clueless surrounding her own mortal state up until the very second, he'd opened his mouth to discuss their mortal condition, or lack of one.

"I don't really remember what happened

to me earlier today to be perfectly honest." Mikia starts to explain. "One minute I was taking a walk in the park and someone attacked me and then a few minutes later, I found myself here."

"Well sorry to say, we're all definitely dead and so that means, you're definitely dead too. I'm Titus." Another man in his mid-forties with a large gash in his head rapidly clarifies.

"Yes, and I'm Riccardo, it's a pleasure to meet you all." The first man mentions as he smiles.

"I'm so sorry, you didn't know Mikia." Susan says apologetically as she gently touches Mikia's hand in a soothing manner and offers her a comforting smile. "It must be a total shock."

Mikia nods in agreement. "Yes, being dead will definitely take some getting used to." She replies. "Slightly different from a getting a new hairstyle isn't it? Why are we waiting here though?" Mikia asks. "If we're all dead, shouldn't we go to straight to heaven or hell or something?"

"Some people believe in purgatory." Susan quickly offers with a smile. "Perhaps that's where we are now."

Nothing about the room itself seems to offer any clues as Mikia quickly visually scans the interior with her eyes, just to see if perhaps she'd missed some kind of useful detail that might add more information to what she did and didn't actually already know.

Death and Mikia's current mortal status had come as a total surprise to her and that reality, or lack of human reality would still take some getting used to but a door did sit on the other side of the room that no one inside the room had yet attempted to open or explore and that for Mikia, was an opportunity.

Something useful or helpful might actually reside on the other side of the door, Mikia quietly starts to consider and that something useful might provide her with more information and so the door, definitely should be opened. Further clues that may provide deeper clarity were required, Mikia finally concludes and if she was brave enough to stand up, cross the room and then actually open it, she might be able to find them. Bravery suddenly seems to take Mikia by the hand as she begins to prepare to rise to her feet and approach the door although she was actually very unsure that it would lead to anywhere or that it even could be opened at all.

A discussion about death and how exactly the people inside the room alongside Mikia had died, seems rather inappropriate and very personal to her, so the issues of the door and where the six were right now, holds far greater appeal to Mikia as a focus point. Quite strangely, death for Mikia, now seems such a private matter and somehow, it actually really doesn't feel quite correct to question other people that are technically strangers and not even yet acquaintances as to how exactly they'd all died.

Friendships as Mikia knows, are almost like a bed that one can lie inside along with another person and sometimes the intricate private details which were like a duvet and blankets would be shared and at other times, they wouldn't. At some point, perhaps a discussion about the manner of their deaths would occur but for now, only a skeleton of information had been shared as some very brief introductions had been made and Mikia really didn't like to dig any deeper as such actions would perhaps disturb the gentle equilibrium of new friendships that were in the process of formation. Once acquaintances had been properly formed and more deeply established, more private, personal intimacies could usually be shared but that comfortable shore of friendship, was definitely a million miles away from where Mikia now sat.

"Do you think we should open that door?" Mikia bravely suggests as she suddenly points towards the door. "Then we might find out exactly where we are and why we're here."

Several of the five faces inside the room wore fearful expressions as Mikia cast a quick glance over each one as her eyes began to search for some kind of agreement but her enthusiasm and curiosity on this occasion it appears, certainly weren't infectious. The door was only a few steps away and so technically, Mikia could easily reach it and then open it but support of some kind was being actively sought out first as she really didn't want to open the door and step through it on her own as there was no telling what might lie on the other side.

"I'm Carlos." A short stocky man suddenly chips in. "And just like all of you, I'm dead too." He rapidly confirms.

Rather amusingly and very surprisingly for Mikia, despite his rather short looking form, Carlos's voice is exceptionally loud for such a tiny man and as each word booms out across the room, Mikia flashes a discreet grin at Susan as she attempts to hold back her giggles. Once Carlos has introduced himself, he quickly begins to dive into some jokes and Mikia manages to temporarily hold herself back from her quest of discovery and the door as she starts to listen to him speak.

Some of the jokes Carlos presents are a million miles away from funny but he seems to possess an endless stream of them as Mikia gives him polite encouraging nods at regular intervals as she silently appreciates his attempts to lighten the mood inside the room. Although Carlos definitely appears to lack competence when it comes to the issue of humour, Mikia at least appreciates his enthusiasm and his efforts to entertain everyone as he manages to reduce the tension inside the room, albeit very slightly.

The mystery of how such a tiny man can speak so loudly however, still remains completely and utterly unsolved as Mikia waits patiently and silently for Carlos to finish and avoids any interruptions. For at least the next twenty minutes, Carlos continues at full speed and maximum capacity as he zooms through pointless joke after joke with no signs of a stoppage or need for an actual breather. During Carlos's verbal race, Mikia spends most of her time in deep deliberation as she holds an internal silent debate over his size and the loudness of his voice, both of which seem to totally contradict one another and an anomaly that is almost absolutely impossible to actually believe as that is slightly more interesting for her than most of his jokes.

Inside the room, Mikia notices that just one woman remains who has not yet spoken but due to Carlos's verbal domination, she can fully appreciate her lack of contributions to the discussion. A polite friendly smile is given to the woman as Mikia attempts to offer her some form of encouragement but there is absolutely no response to Mikia's efforts. In fact, the woman's face remains totally stagnant, unflinchingly unresponsive, completely stiff and extremely still but in all that stillness, a very downcast expression sits very evidently upon it.

To plaster a smile across that face Carlos would definitely have to improve his jokes and that reality was absolutely undeniable as Mikia could very clearly see. Regardless of the introductions and efforts that had been made by everyone else inside the room, the woman's facial expression and attitude did not seem to waver and ten minutes later, when Carlos finally decides to take a break and pause, Mikia notices that she still hasn't made any effort at all to join the conversation and she starts to doubt that she ever will.

"My death was a complete surprise. I was totally unprepared for it and I'm still in shock really." The woman suddenly mourns as she sadly shakes her head. "I'm Melinda." She mentions.

From Mikia's lips a sigh relief almost escapes as she glances at Melinda's face and then gives her an understanding nod and encouraging smile as she welcomes the fact that Melinda's silence is now broken. In many ways as Mikia is still dealing with her own shock, she can definitely appreciate and certainly relate to Melinda's position and point of view which seem much closer to her own experiences that day. The frankness of Melinda's comment starts to resonate very deeply with Mikia's own sentiments as when she'd woken up earlier that morning, death was the last person that she'd expected to meet and even now, acceptance that death had paid her an actual visit was a hard reality to fully accept.

"I guess that's one thing we all have in common." Carlos jokes. "We're all dead."

Very unfortunately and rather sadly, Carlos's totally inappropriate, very tactless joke rapidly struck Mikia's heart with a hard, sharp blow as that awful reality ran around inside her thoughts like a speeding train that was just about to crash. Nothing but an awkward, uncomfortable silence sat in-between the occupants of the room as Mikia silently began to process and digest the truth that no one could possibly deny, least of all herself. From what Mikia could see as she cast a quick thoughtful glance around the room, no actual smiles were given in response to Carlos's joke as each word sank reluctantly deeper into her thoughts and almost began to consume her.

"I wonder why there's only six of us here." Susan suddenly mentions as she glances at some of the empty chairs that line the walls of the room.

"Yes, isn't that strange?" Mikia rapidly agrees as she welcomes the conversational change of direction.

"Why bother to have all these empty chairs if only six of us are here." Susan concludes. "It's very strange isn't it?"

"Perhaps they didn't have a smaller room." Titus offers as he grins. "I say, we should open up the door and then step right through it."

"Now that kind of thinking Titus is what gave you that wound on your head." Carlos jokes sarcastically. "I'm staying put right here. You want to open that door and then actually walk through it, you go for it, I'll watch."

"Do you think it could be dangerous?" Mikia asks as she turns to face Susan.

"I don't know but I don't really care if it is, it has to be better than sitting here all day and night." Susan insists with a smile. "I mean, we could be stuck here for a week, a month, a year or even for eternity."

"I don't think I can stand Carlos's jokes for another week." Titus teases with a sarcastic grin. "That would be a minute too long."

Mikia giggles.

Suddenly the door of the room, very unexpectedly, actually flies open and Mikia immediately turns to face it as she holds her breath and waits in an almost fearful silence for whoever or whatever is about to step inside the room. A quick glance at the others inside the room rapidly confirms to Mikia that everyone else around her is also caught by surprise as some fearful gasps actually manage to escape from some of their lips.

Someone or something was indeed just about to enter inside the room and no one present it appears to Mikia has the slightest notion of who exactly that someone was, or what they would do when

14

they were indeed actually present. A blanket of fear suddenly falls over the room as panic starts to reign but Mikia notices that it's a silent, unspoken panic that resides deep inside everyone's thoughts. Fearful expressions adorn all of the faces of those around Mikia which do not require any words to be understandable and every remnant of frivolity and soothing amusement it appears has now, rapidly vanished.

Just an empty second or two goes by before a very mature man that looks to be at least ninety years old, makes his way inside the room and then stands just in front of the now open door. Upon his face there is a warm smile which immediately puts the occupants of the room at ease again and as they start to relax, they wait in a slightly more pleasant silence for him to speak.

"Greetings everyone." The man announces with a beaming smile. "I work for the Bureau of Death and for now, you've all been assigned to the Reconciliation Team. You are all now dead as you may be aware and since you have been specially selected to form part of this team, you will all be trained to assume your assigned roles and to perform the duties that your role requires."

"How and when did this happen?" Carlos demands as he quickly interrupts. "How did we get assigned? What if we don't wish to be assigned?"

"I'm afraid Carlos, you don't have any choice." The man quickly clarifies. "The Bureau of Death governs the afterlife and Death, who leads the Bureau, allocates every soul that is collected according to their strengths and weaknesses. This is a duty not a choice. I hate to break the sad news to you Carlos but rather unfortunately, your access to choices and free will actually die along with your physical human body."

"Really?" Carlos asks in total disbelief. "Is this for real, I thought we'd at least get to go to heaven or hell."

"No Carlos that only happens to those who believe in such things and you only get to experience that luxury or nightmare, if your services are not required by the Bureau." He explains. "My name is Restoration and I'm one of Death's assistants but a very senior member of the Bureau, so if you have any questions, you can direct them to me." Restoration adds as he turns to face everyone else inside the room and then smiles.

Quite interesting for Mikia, every part of Restoration's form as she quietly began to absorb and inspect his appearance slightly more closely, was slightly contradictory but strangely rather soothing. Each of the words that left Restoration's mouth would float gently across the room like a warm summer breeze, even though some of the news he brought along with him actually had some quite negative implications.

The nature of Restoration's soothing words and his comforting tone however, were extremely calm and very peaceful but almost every inch of his form was draped in black robes as if he'd just attended a funeral ceremony, Mikia observes. A strange air of authority was present and it was almost as if his whole aura sent a silent demand for respect to the entire room without even the verbal expression or exchange of a single tense word.

"So, we never go to heaven?" Titus asks.

"If your soul can be fully restored through your reconciliation work for the Bureau of Death and once it is felt that you have done enough, you might get to retire to Rest in Peace." Restoration immediately clarifies. "If you're no longer required. Heaven and hell are only for those who really believe in them or that immediately qualify and your souls need some restoration work, so they weren't pure enough for heaven or evil and corrupt enough for hell and Rest in Peace is kind of alternative eternity."

"Sounds very complicated." Susan mentions.

"This actually works out in your favour. Before we established the Rest in Peace alternative and the Restoration Process, if there was any doubt at all, Death would just throw souls straight

into hell, so this is a compromise."
Restoration points out reassuringly as
he elaborates. "And a rather decent one
if I might say so myself."

"So, we'd all be in hell right now?"
Carlos asks.

"Yes, and you'd all be rather hot."
Restoration mentions as he nods. "It's
not very nice down there and the heat is
absolutely unbearable."

"Okay, I can live with that." Carlos
replies.

"Actually, you can't Carlos because
you're dead." Restoration mentions.
"Which means you'll have to be dead with
that."

Carlos shrugs.

"See Carlos, he's actually funny."
Titus teases as he grins.

Once Restoration seems satisfied that
there are no further questions to be
asked, he suddenly starts to prepare
himself to leave which catches Mikia off
guard slightly as she'd held an
expectation that he would present for a
while. Just as Mikia had begun to feel
quite comfortable with Restoration's
presence, it quickly transpires that it
was not going to be permanent, or even
last very long at all and as she watches
him turn and face the door, a sudden
flurry of questions starts to occupy her
mind as panic rapidly starts to set in.
Inside Mikia's mind, she starts to
silently wonder if she's actually missed
her opportunity to present her questions
to Restoration as she watches him as he

doesn't seem to be very keen on hanging around.

A part of Mikia suddenly starts to feel completely frozen as her tongue rapidly ties itself up in fearful knots which seem to hold every word captive firmly behind her lips as Restoration starts to vanish. Nothing but silence and stillness however surround Mikia as everyone else inside the room just sits and watches Restoration depart without any objections at all.

"You wanted to ask me a question Mikia?" Restoration suddenly enquires as he quickly steps back inside the room and then pauses just beside the door.

The lack of words spoken on Mikia's part strangely seems totally irrelevant as she casts a quizzical glance towards Restoration's face and confusion rapidly starts to swirl around inside her thoughts. Now there were even more questions inside Mikia's mind as she hadn't even said a single word and it almost appears as if Restoration can actually read her mind. Truthfully, Mikia had more than one question that she really wanted to ask but confusion ran rampant through her thoughts as she internally began to try and decide which one was the most appropriate and the most important as nervous fear clung to every part of her being.

"Don't worry Mikia, you can ask me absolutely anything you want to." Restoration quickly reassures her.

"Can you read our minds?" Mikia

immediately asks.

"Yes, which can actually be quite helpful sometimes but a real pain at other times." Restoration replies. "As some people's thoughts, you'd really rather not know about at all."

"You see Carlos that was a proper joke." Titus teases as he gives Carlos a sarcastic smile.

"Will there be any more people joining us Restoration?" Mikia enquires.

"Not for now. This is just your restoration group and once you've successfully resolved your own deaths, settled any issues with loved ones, sorted out your imperfections and made any amends with the living, you'll either stay in this group and become a reconciliation team, or be allocated to another group." Restoration explains. "Or you could even transcend to Rest in Peace which is where most souls go when their souls have been fully restored and their work for the Bureau is done."

"What happens if our souls are never restored?" Carlos asks.

"If it is deemed impossible to restore your soul and your work for the Bureau isn't productive, after a probation period of six months, Death sends you to hell." Restoration explains. "That doesn't happen often though as most people are redeemable."

"How long will we be in this group?" Mikia asks.

"Well that depends really on how long it takes each of you to restore your soul." Restoration explains. "The restoration of each individual soul is a very personal issue and it's not actually something that you can achieve as a team." He adds. "You can assist and support each other but the final restoration is a very individual achievement."

"Separation soon might actually be a good thing." Titus mentions playfully. "Carlos's jokes are so bad, I can't be dead with him and them for a whole eternity.

"Jealousy is not a very attractive quality Titus." Carlos replies curtly.

"What happens to us now?" Mikia asks.

"You'll find out soon enough." Restoration insists as he smiles and then turns to face the door. "I don't want to spoil all the surprises that would be really quite mean of me."

"You see Carlos, he's very funny." Titus teases as he laughs. "Restoration, we need you to reconcile and restore Carlos's lack of funnability to spare our souls and our minds."

Just a few seconds later, the door closes behind Restoration and as the six are once more left alone inside the room with only each other. They glance at each other's faces as they wait nervously and expectantly for what is due to occur next in total silence as nervous anticipation starts to fill them. Mysterious activities were due to commence but Restoration hadn't provided any further details as to what exactly those activities would comprise off and so uncertainty began to silently reign inside the room.

Fortunately, Restoration's rather sudden departure did put an abrupt end to Carlos and Titus's sarcastic bickering as the two men fell completely silent and sat totally still, so that they could lick their wounds from their quite negative verbal exchanges. Another ten silent, rather tense minutes went rather slowly by as the occupants inside the room held onto their tongues in expectant hopeful anticipation as they gave Restoration's words further internal due consideration. Every set of eyes inside the room did not waver or move even a single inch as the door which also remained completely still, became a focal point for each of the room's occupants.

"He wasn't around for very long." Carlos finally jokes as he suddenly breaks the silence inside the room.

"Perhaps he doesn't like hanging around with dead people." Titus replies as he grins.

"Look Titus, since we're going to be around each other for a while we should really try to call a truce." Carlos suggests diplomatically.

"Sure, a temporary ceasefire sounds good to me, at least until we're out of this place." Titus agrees. "But I can't make any promises about the forever thing if we get stuck together for eternity because I really can't

commit to unrealistic goals of
everlasting patience. My soul just
isn't in that place yet."

"A temporary ceasefire will do."
Carlos immediately reassures him. "I'm
easy to please."

"I don't think we'll ever get out of
this room." Riccardo suddenly mentions.
"Seriously, we've been in here for
ages."

"Maybe even a year." Susan suggests
as she giggles. "How does time go by in
this place? Is it even the same?"

"You know, you do have a valid point
Susan." Mikia agrees. "The passage of
time here could be totally different."

A minute later, the door suddenly
swings open again and a woman steps
inside the room that looks very much
like Restoration in the sense that every
inch of her attire is black. An
external black robe hangs from her frame
in a pretty similar manner although
there is a slightly more elegant black
dress underneath it. Everyone inside
the room immediately stares at her and
keeps completely silent as they wait for
her to speak.

"If you'd all like to follow me
please?" She requests as she smiles.
"I'm just here to get you started. My
name is Serenity."

"Where are we actually going
Serenity?" Carlos asks as he quickly
rises to his feet. "Though to be
perfectly honest, I'd go anywhere with
you." He teases playfully.

"Godfrey is waiting for you all, just outside." Serenity explains. "This is very serious Carlos, you are being prepared for your duties and the restoration of your soul and neither of those matters can be taken lightly."

"Right." Carlos replies with a grin. "At least you know my name though, so I'm happy."

"I know everyone's name Carlos, it's my job. You should try to bear in mind that life and death are not a laughing matter and the issues that arise can be very serious indeed. You need to prepare yourself for that if you wish to be a productive and respectful soul." Serenity advises. "Is everyone ready?" She asks as she turns to face the rest of the group.

Mikia immediately nods in response. "Yes, I guess I'm ready." She replies.

"I'm not entirely sure that anyone can truly ever be ready but once you arrive here, you're as ready as you can be really, so don't worry about it too much Mikia." Serenity explains as she starts to lead the six towards the door.

"Where are we actually going with Godfrey?" Carlos asks.

"First of all, you will revisit your lives, so that you can reconcile your own lives and deaths." Serenity explains. "Then once you have done that you'll have to attend to your own personal matters, sort out your imperfections, make amends and so on."

"When do we join the Reconciliation

Team?" Susan asks. "How do we reconcile our lives and deaths?"

"This all sounds like it could take a very long time." Carlos says as he gently shakes his head.

"You'll understand more when you return." Serenity insists.

"We won't be doing anything dangerous will we?" Carlos presses as he discreetly attempts to extract more information from Serenity before he actually exits the room.

"Carlos, your physical body has now been disposed of which means, only your soul remains which also means, no one can physically hurt you anymore." Serenity immediately reassures him. "You're quite safe here and you'll be in very safe hands, Godfrey is one of our best afterlife guides."

A soft musical lilt was present in Serenity's tone which was not harsh or hard at all that began to lift Mikia's spirit and encourage her. Questions began to scurry through Mikia's thoughts however as to whether or not Serenity was actually an angel or some kind of celestial being but her lips were reluctant to ask any unnecessary questions that for now, would make absolutely no difference to Mikia's current situation at all. Answers would not change the fact that Mikia had died that day and from what she'd been told, she already knew, she would definitely have other opportunities and enough time to ask such questions at some point in the future and so verbal hesitation on this occasion was an acceptable form of action to take.

"Ready everybody?" Serenity asks as she urges and encourages the group to depart.

"Yes." Susan replies as she starts to walk towards the door.

"I'm ready." Carlos agrees as he quickly follows her.

Several things seem to happen all at once as Mikia starts to walk towards the door and then actually steps through it as the hallway that she enters into suddenly starts to spin, faster and faster until everything around her becomes a blur. Everyone around Mikia begins to sway from side to side as they rapidly hold onto each other's arms and giggle as the sensation that they can feel from the motion and movement is quite pleasant and not scary in any way and Mikia giggles as she joins in the frivolity.

Everything that surrounds Mikia suddenly turns a brilliant white and just a few seconds later, the brilliant white light starts to fade and as it does so, the six immediately find themselves sat upon some seats in the back of a rather strange looking rather large taxi. In the driver's seat, at the very front of the taxi which has a separation partition that is open, a man that looks to be in his late fifties can be seen and he suddenly turns to face them all and gives them a large, friendly grin as he nods.

Rather mysteriously, Serenity has by this point, completely disappeared but when and how that actually happened, Mikia is unsure as she didn't even say goodbye. In the larger scheme of things however, Mikia quickly decides that it doesn't actually seem to matter as the taxi driver it appears has been waiting for them to arrive and he now seems anxious to make a start on their very mysterious journey.

2 ROMNEY'S FALL

To be updated

3 DIGNITY DEMANDS A VERDICT

To be updated

RECONCILIATIONS

4 MASKED MAYHEM

To be updated

5 DISTURBED

To be updated

6 SUSAN'S SCARS

To be updated

7 MIRRORS & REFLECTIONS

To be updated

8 A HUNDRED FACES

To be updated

9 STAIRWAY OF TRIALS

To be updated

10 RECONCILIATIONS

To be updated